Nathan Davis
303 7th St
Bucoda, Wa,

Michel's Mixed-Up Musical Bird

Michel's Mixed-Up Musical Bird

by Michel Legrand and George Mendoza

Illustrations by
DePatie-Freleng Enterprises, Inc.

THE BOBBS-MERRILL COMPANY, INC.
Indianapolis   New York

Thanks are extended to American Broadcasting Companies, Inc., for the use of its program title, ABC AFTERSCHOOL SPECIALS, on which the program "Michel's Mixed-Up Musical Bird" has appeared.

Published by The Bobbs-Merrill Company, Inc.
Indianapolis   New York

Manufactured in the United States of America
First printing

Library of Congress Cataloging in Publication Data

Legrand, Michel, 1932–
  Michel's mixed-up musical bird.
  SUMMARY: The adventures of a young boy and the mischievous bird
he rescues from a storm.
  [1. Birds—Fiction]   I.   Mendoza, George, joint author.
II. DePatie-Freleng Enterprises.   III.   Title.
PZ7.L5213Mi   [Fic]   77–15448
ISBN 0–672–52396–5

For Eugenie and Benjamin,
who first heard the story . . .
and with special thanks
to Helen Sweetland and
Squire D. Rushnell

The beginning I remember very well. . . .

I was only a boy then, with a dream of becoming a composer. I was no more than fifteen, a very serious student of music at the Paris Conservatory, living at our small country house a short scooter-ride away.

It was late spring. I remember I had gone for a walk to a village nearby to think about what I was going to create for the composition I needed to pass my examination. Sometimes walking through the countryside would lift me out of my shoes, and many ideas would come to me.

On my way back home, I noticed that all kinds of buds and flowers were stirring. I breathed deeply the smells of the woods coming to life once more. Nature knows when to begin, I thought, and when to end. Nature is full of musical ideas under leaves, around ponds, high up in the trees, everywhere. All you have to do is stand still and close your eyes and listen to the castanets of the crickets, the choir of flutes in the wind, the mingling melodies of all kinds of birds, and the rhythmic gribbet, gribbet of the lowly frog.

For a moment I stood like a tree in the forest, wishing I could be like nature, when suddenly the sky darkened, the air filled with drumrolls of thunder, and whiptails of lightning flashed down at me.

Then it began to rain, great pourings of rain mixed with more lightning and thunder.

I had to make a run for it, since it was dangerous being close to the trees, with the lightning flaring around me. How I wished I were safely inside my warm house, with dry clothes on, and Madame Footy preparing my favorite peppermint tea with honey.

As I was running down the dirt road that led to my house, a daggerlike flash struck a tree ahead of me, and a huge limb came crashing to the ground, blocking my path.

I had started to scramble over the twisted branch when I noticed a nest tangled in the broken boughs and heard the cries of a frightened bird.

Caught under the full rage of the storm, I made my way carefully toward the crying bird. Inside the nest there was a little head, a little beak, so tiny a bird, with its black eyes peering up at me from a ball of soaked feathers.

Reaching down into the nest, I scooped out the baby bird very gently, and with the rain beating down on us, I tried to console the helpless creature that trembled in my hands.

"Don't be afraid, little fellow," I said, stroking his head. "I'm not going to hurt you."

Just then a flood of lightning filled the forest, and I thought I saw a huge hawk looking down at us from another tree.

"I don't see your mother," I said. "But I think we have an unfriendly character watching us."

The bird began to cry again, and I tried to calm him, with the rain running across my glasses. "Don't be afraid; don't be afraid. I'm not going to leave you here. You are coming home with me. . . ."

Then, tucking the bird safely inside my jacket pocket, I made straight for my house, while the thunder rolled, the lightning flashed, and the rain continued to fall from the sky.

When I reached the door, Madame Footy was already there, waiting to open it for me. Oh, she was a character, I can tell you that. A combination housekeeper and grand-mère, she was always concerned about me and my studies.

But how she fussed over her cats! Jacques and Claude, as she called them, were like her babies, and you could see them always necking 'round her legs, trying to charm her when it suited them or when they wanted something from her.

And, oh, they hated to share her affections! So whenever Madame Footy was annoyed with me, you could hear them purring out their pleasure.

Now you can imagine their wide-eyed amusement as they looked on while I stood dripping into my puddle on Madame Footy's spotless floor, my hair plastered all over my face and Madame Footy scolding me about playing in the rain like a child when I should be studying my music lessons.

Trying to explain anything to Madame Footy was useless, so I remained quiet until my poor little bird uttered a loud cry.

"What is that?" asked Madame Footy, pinching her eyes toward me.

"A bird," I said, taking out the half-drowned creature. "The storm has made him an orphan."

"A bird!" She jumped back. "A filthy, dirty bird! Out of this house with that bird!"

Ah, she was upset. She turned blue, then red, under her white hair. But I was stubborn and insisted we care for the creature.

"We?" said Madame Footy. "*We* will do nothing of the kind."

"Then I will do it. I will be his—or her—father."

"You're going to bring disease upon us all with that bird," she warned, with her finger raised to my nose. Then she turned to Jacques and Claude, who were both eyeing the bird with relish. "You keep away from that filthy bird! Do you hear me?"

"He's just a baby, Madame Footy," I said. "He needs someone to take care of him until he is strong enough to be on his own."

"What about your studies, your examination?" Madame Footy's words mingled with a duet of reowwws from Jacques and Claude as I took my bird upstairs. "You haven't started your composition, and here you are wasting your time on a bird, turning our house into an animal shelter. What is going to become of you, Michel?" Madame Footy's voice faded as she moved toward the kitchen to get her mop to clean up the puddled floor.

Once inside my room, I wrapped the baby bird in a soft towel.

"You're shivering," I said. "Your mother must be worried about you. If only she knew I was taking care of you and that you are not alone somewhere out in that storm."

The bird gave out a piccolo chirp that sounded as though he agreed with me.

"Now you stay there while I change into some dry clothes myself," I said. And once more the bird answered with his tiny "tweet-tweet."

"Is that the only note you know?" I asked my little friend, who replied again with his one-note cry.

"I have the perfect name for you," I said. "One-Note. Well, what do you think about that?"

Cocking his head the way birds do when they want to observe you closely, One-Note chirped his note. He approved.

But then I began to think, What am I going to do with
him? How ... where ...? I knew I had to protect him—or
"her." I don't know; I think it was "him." I don't know
why.

Suddenly I saw the curious faces of Jacques and Claude
peering into my room, and as I shouted at them to keep
away, I realized that I had to build a birdhouse without a
moment's delay.

Digging through my closet, I found an old brass cage
buried beneath toys and discarded musical instruments.
It was a terrible mess, with missing bars, and I remember
it had no perch or swing. It was much too shabby for my
little One-Note.

I must use my imagination, I thought, and rebuild this
birdcage to make it a safe and worthy place for One-Note
to live in.

"I am going to make your house not only *catproof*," I announced, looking down at One-Note, who seemed content inside the nest of my towel, "but musical as well!"

And so, improvising with parts of musical instruments, this is what I did to make One-Note a catproof, musical birdhouse:

I used the strings from a toy violin to replace the missing bars. A trombone slide became a perch, and the mute from a trumpet filled the need for a feeding dish.

I seem to recall that a piece of a baton was strung from two guitar strings to form a swing. I am not sure how I used an abandoned piano key, but it served some kind of purpose, I am sure.

When it was all finished, I stepped back to admire my creation. "No other bird in all the world can claim such a house," I said to One-Note with great pride. "What more could a baby bird want?"

9.

But as soon as One-Note was inside his cage, he began screaming loudly.

"Of course, poor thing, you must be starving!"

I knew that small birds couldn't swallow—that I knew. So, I decided to try something. I wet a little bit of bread in some milk, and with my finger I pushed the bread deep down inside One-Note's throat. And it seemed to work. So several times a day I was feeding him this way.

And as the days passed, I came to feel as though I were truly One-Note's father. I was feeding him, talking to him, playing with him, defending him against Madame Footy, and protecting him from Jacques and Claude.

And as spring turned soft and green in the fields and woods, One-Note grew into a radiant black-feathered magpie. During that time I ignored my studies and thought only of looking after my little friend.

But now I had to try to finish my badly neglected composition.

Of course, One-Note had other ideas. After all, he had no examinations to pass.

One day when I was working at the piano, One-Note perched himself on the windowsill beside me. Every time I struck a note or a chord, One-Note started to chirp wildly away.

I tried to put the notes down on my scoring paper, but it was very difficult for me to concentrate on what I was doing. Finally I said, "Oh, One-Note, can't you see that I'm trying to finish my composition? And you're not helping me with all that noise. I just can't think."

One-Note stopped chirping and gave me one of his quizzical looks that seemed to say, "Stop that nonsense and come play with me."

But I couldn't. I was behind in my studies, and Madame Footy was angry enough about that. I told One-Note to go and play with Robespierre, our old dog, who lay sleeping in the yard beneath the window.

Poor Robespierre!

One-Note jumped down from the windowsill onto Robespierre's back, and with his talons gripping flesh and hair, he rooted himself there.

Robespierre sprang into the air. He bucked and growled as he tried to shake One-Note off his back. He turned round and round, trying to snap at One-Note, but he couldn't rid himself of the pesky bird.

Robespierre's frantic yowling and One-Note's cocky chirping made such a commotion that I couldn't resist leaving the piano to watch them from the window. What an opera. How I laughed as One-Note rode Robespierre like a rodeo star, up and down, up and down all over the yard, with Robespierre trying to buck him off.

Finally One-Note decided to let himself be thrown back up onto the windowsill.

Madame Footy heard the commotion and was furious. Adding her voice to the chorus, she ordered me to get back to my studies at once.

As I returned reluctantly to my work, I looked at One-Note, who had hopped onto the top of the piano.

You are curious and restless, too, I thought. You and I are filled with the same spirit for life and adventure.

It was that time for both of us—that time before you suddenly grow up and have to fly out into the real world.

My thoughts were interrupted when One-Note uttered a complaining tweet.

"Are you scolding me too?" I smiled and began working again on my composition.

Each time I played a few experimental notes of a melody or a chord and then turned to put them down on my scoring pad, One-Note hopped a little closer to the paper. At first, he looked at the paper with puzzled interest. Then he tried to pick off the little black specks with his beak, as though they were seeds to eat.

What a ridiculous bird! He made me laugh as he continued to try to eat my music. But he seemed so determined that I decided it was time for One-Note to have a music lesson.

I tried to explain that notes were not birdseed at all, but dots of ink, each related to a key on the piano. He chirped and then began to peck away some more.

"No, no, silly bird!" I said. "Let me show you with a scale."

I got out a blank sheet of music paper and quickly wrote out a simple scale. As I played the scale and sang "do-re-mi-fa-so-la-ti-do," I pointed to each note on the paper with my other hand.

One-Note watched closely, and I quickly discovered that he was an eager student. When I reached the last note of the scale, One-Note chirped along.

Smiling with delight, I praised One-Note, who proudly chirped the note again.

I laughed. "Lucky for you that the last note of the scale was *your* note!"

But then One-Note surprised me.

Hopping down onto the piano keyboard, he surveyed the keys. Then, leaning down, he pecked the last note of the scale.

"Very good! If you practiced a little each day, you might become the first bird to play Chopin," I said, grinning from ear to ear.

After that, One-Note displayed his musical virtuosity by chirping along with my playing or by standing on the keyboard and finishing off scales for me. Sometimes, when I tried to trick him by striking the wrong note of a scale, he even supplied the correct note with a tap of his beak on the key.

One-Note was truly a musical bird, and he showed definite tastes in music. When I played Schubert and Chopin,

oh, how he would chirp away. But when I played Bach
one day, he screeched his little heart out until I had to
stop. Then he did something I will never forget. He hopped
over to the music sheet and began to tear it into small pieces
with his beak.

I couldn't believe my eyes. He was attacking my music
sheet, attacking it savagely, shredding it as though it were
a piece of lettuce.

"One-Note, STOP!" I cried.

One-Note backed away suddenly, and accidentally slipped off the edge of the piano.

"Why didn't you fly?" I said, gathering him up from the floor.

Then I realized why. "You don't know how, do you? You've never had anyone to teach you."

One-Note looked at me and chirped a questioning "tweet?"

"I will teach you, One-Note. It has come time for you to learn to fly."

I took One-Note out to the field behind our house for his first flying lesson. Holding him toward the sky, I released him. But he fluttered helplessly to earth. I tried several times, but he was very confused. I wasn't quite sure how I was going to get him airborne.

Madame Footy looked on with dismay as I set One-Note on a tree stump and instructed him to stay there and watch me. Robespierre woke up and gazed at us from under a bush.

"Now you have to flap your wings," I said, "like this . . ." And I began running around the field, flapping my arms as though I were a bird ready to take off into the sky.

"You see, One-Note?" I cried. "You can do it. You can fly."

And for a moment I thought how wonderful it would be to lift off into the clouds, to fly above the trees, to feel the glory of a simple bird.

All of a sudden, I caught sight of the stealthy figures of Jacques and Claude, preparing to pounce on One-Note.

"One-Note! Look out!" I screamed just as the cats rushed him at the same time from opposite sides.

Miraculously, by a whisker of fate, One-Note flapped his wings and lifted into the air, barely escaping the cats' deadly claws.

All kinds of buds and flowers were stirring.

...*a little head,*
a little beak,
so tiny a bird...

Ah, Madame Footy was upset.

"*No other bird in all the world can claim such a house.*"

One-Note grew into a radiant black-feathered magpie.

And then suddenly he was going up, up and up, gliding higher into the sky. He was as weightless as a dream inside a cloud, his feathers like the petals of a flower brushing the air.

I watched my bird as he circled high above the trees, swooping and curving his wings against the surging currents of wind. I wondered how the world looked to him up there, with people and animals fastened to the earth below him.

Would he come back to me? Or would he fly away forever and forget me?

"One-Note," I called out, waving to him, "come back!"

Madame Footy looked very concerned as she followed One-Note's first journey above the earth. Robespierre barked wildly toward the sky, and even the cats looked up as One-Note explored the endless reaches of open space.

I was feeling very sad, thinking I had seen the last of him, when down he came, like a streak out of the sun, dive-bombing Jacques and Claude.

"What a rascal you are!" I said as the cats scattered for their lives.

Then One-Note flew down and perched on my head. Although he was breathing very hard, he managed to sing his one-note song, proud as he could be.

Now that One-Note knew how to fly, he followed me overhead as I made my daily trips to the conservatory.

What a wonderful way to begin the day, I thought, as One-Note flew a foot or so above my head while I scootered to the main road that led to Paris. And there, at the end of our country lane, he would fly up into a tree. I would say good-by to him, and he would sing his glorious morning song back to me.

When I returned from school, One-Note would be waiting for me in the same tree at the end of the woods.

One morning as I was saying good-by to One-Note, I saw a hawk floating silently through the sky. He was drifting in slow circles under the clouds, and I worried about One-Note on my way to school and all during the day.

One-Note could trick the cats and provoke Robespierre, and he was smart enough to know how to tap out the piano scales with his beak, but a hawk—that was different; that was the real world.

I tried to concentrate on my studies, but my mind kept wandering out into the woods with One-Note. . . .

"What are you dreaming about today?" asked my professor. "All the time you are looking out the window. Will you find your music out there in the trees? Is the summer sky going to finish your composition for you? Michel, Michel . . . you are wasting your natural gifts!"

After school that day I realized that I was devoting too much time to One-Note and only a spoonful of my energies to my studies. I resolved to complete my composition, but it was really One-Note who helped me do it.

One morning he woke me early, singing as I had never heard him sing before. I tried to ignore him by burrowing under the covers, but he was determined to get me out of bed.

"Yah—you are a pest this morning," I said, my eyes still half-closed. "Please, One-Note, please let me sleep just a little bit longer. . . ."

But it was no use. One-Note wanted to play. That bird always wanted to play.

"I cannot play with you now!" I scolded. "I have to work. Have you never heard that word?"

Opening his shiny beak, One-Note poured out his song to me. . . .

"Twe-e-e-et, twe-e-e-et, tweet-tweet," he sang, until the whole house seemed to be filled with his original one-note music.

"You are full of inspiring sounds today," I said. "Why don't you go to the piano and compose?"

When I got to the piano, One-Note was already there, chirping and singing even more intensely than before, "Twe-e-e-et, twe-e-e-et, tweet-tweet . . ."

And while I did not realize it at the time, I began composing my piece based on One-Note's single expressive "tweet." For, you see, while it was only one note, my talented bird had a wondrous way of making it softer and louder, longer and shorter, faster and slower. It was a challenge, but it could be done. After all, if Ravel could compose a whole piano concerto for one hand, I could compose a little piece based on one note.

So there we were, actually composing together, and when it was finished I called it *Fantasia* by One-Note and Michel Legrand.

"Well, my friend, we did it!" I said, turning to One-Note, my collaborator. But he was gone—out to tease Jacques and Claude again!

Besides having an enormous talent for music, One-Note had an even greater gift for tricking cats. I don't know how he did it, but somehow he managed to get Madame Footy's spoiled babies into all sorts of messy troubles.

"Shoo! SHOO! Leave them alone, you troublemaker!" Madame Footy's voice rang out from the yard.

I rushed outside in time to see the cats leap up at One-Note, who was perched on the rim of the rain barrel.

46

Just at that precise moment the cunning bird flew up, escaping the cats' paws, while Jacques and Claude went over the rim of the barrel, tumbling headlong into the water!

"I've had enough of that bird," Madame Footy said as she plucked her cats out of the barrel. I couldn't help laughing at Jacques and Claude, who now looked like two skinned fish.

"You have been busy this morning," I said to One-Note as he chirped away on top of my head. "But enough of your games. I must hurry. I don't want to be late to class today, because our composition is finally finished."

When I submitted *Fantasia* to my professor, he was so delighted that he gave it the highest mark he could bestow on a composition. But he was somewhat bewildered by my collaborator's credit.

"What is this, 'One-Note'?" he asked.

"Part of the creation," I answered humbly.

"I see. . . . Actually I don't see . . . but no matter. You've done something very original, and I'm proud of you, Michel."

Madame Footy would be proud too, I thought, but I really wanted to hurry home so that I could tell One-Note about our triumph at the conservatory.

When I returned from school, One-Note was not waiting for me in his tree at the end of the woods.

I called out to him several times, but he did not answer.

Then, to my horror, I saw three black wing feathers at the foot of the tree.

I looked around desperately, searching the woods
for a sign of him, whistling our theme from *Fantasia*.
"Twe-e-e-et, twe-e-e-et, tweet-tweet." But there was no
answer.

Rushing home, I asked Madame Footy if she had seen
One-Note.

"No, I haven't seen him," she said, "but good riddance."

I accused Jacques and Claude, but they meowwed their innocence. I went into the village and asked the shopkeepers if they had seen One-Note. I searched the woods once more.

There was no sign of One-Note anywhere.

My heart felt broken. I returned home and played our theme on the piano. Over and over I played it and, I remember, that night I couldn't sleep. I kept looking out of my window at the stars, praying that One-Note was not lying hurt somewhere, hoping that in the morning he would be singing to me to get up and play with him.

But when morning came, there was still no familiar chirping. A sadness fell upon everyone that day. Even Madame Footy admitted she missed "that bird" and kept looking up at the empty sky.

I think Jacques and Claude missed him too, for they no longer seemed as playful and as mischievous as before.

I didn't know what had happened to him and as the days went by I began to fear I might never see One-Note again.

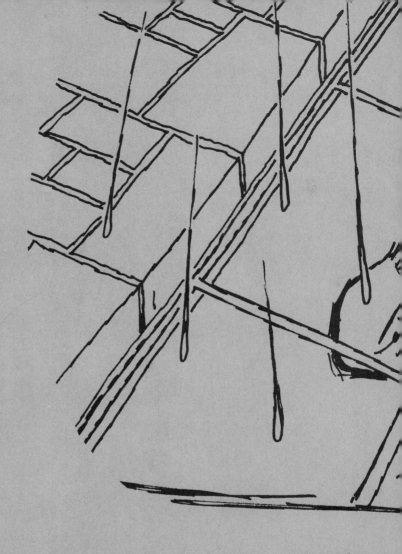

All I could do was wait, I thought, and hope that he would come back to me.

"It's been almost a week, Michel . . . too many days have passed," said Madame Footy.

As I stood looking out the window, I tried to put Madame Footy's words out of my mind. I watched the sky darken and the rain begin to fall, and I remembered that stormy day when I had found One-Note in his fallen nest.

I sat down at the piano and began to play *Fantasia* by picking out the notes slowly with one finger.

Rain fell in hard spurts against the window pane, and as I repeated One-Note's theme, I became aware that it was echoing back from a distance. I must be imagining sounds that are not there, I thought, and I picked out the notes again, this time listening intently.

It was true—the theme echoed back and was growing louder.

"Twe-e-e-et, twe-e-e-et, tweet-tweet."

Jumping up from the piano, I pressed my face to the window. "Oh, One-Note, where are you?" I called.

I could hear him crying somewhere out there in the rain. Rushing for the door, I cried to Madame Footy, "It's One-Note! He's come home!"

Madame Footy and the animals had heard his cry too and were already running for the front door. In a burst of excitement we all ran out into the heavy rain.

Then I saw him, my bird, One-Note, struggling to walk, hobbling along on the ground, obviously injured, crying out wildly. I feared the worst. . . .

"One-Note! One-Note!" I shouted as I ran to help him. But when I reached him, I saw—oh, it was terrible! His wings had been twisted and torn, and he was unable to fly.

Picking him up, I cradled him in my hands with all the tenderness I knew. "Who would have done such a cruel thing to you?" my heart cried out.

One-Note jumped down from the windowsill onto Robespierre's back.

He rode Robespierre like a rodeo st

One-Note showed definite tastes in music.

One-Note slipped off the edge of the piano.

"Now you have to flap your wings," I said, "like this . . ."

But a hawk . . . that was the real world.

His wings had been twisted and torn.

"It looks as though he has been attacked by a hawk," said Madame Footy, leading us back through the rain.

I stroked his head for a long time, trying to calm him down. Then I took him to his musical house where he would be safe.

"I will protect you; don't be afraid; don't be afraid," I kept trying to reassure him.

But for many days and nights he squawked like mad. It was as though he were a baby all over again, and I had to care for him just as I had done when I rescued him from the forest storm.

Until the end of that summer, we all cared for One-Note and slowly, very slowly, his wing feathers began to grow back. We watched him as he worked and worked on his feathers, preening them with his beak, sometimes for hours at a time.

How determined he was to fly again! His determination both fascinated and inspired us all. Even Jacques and Claude seemed to encourage him to fly once more. After all, a cat's life is very boring without a bird to chase.

Then one day, when his wings were shiny and whole again, we all went outside, wondering if he would fly. Were his new wings strong enough to lift him into the sky?

I stroked his head and blew softly against his feathers.

"Don't be afraid," I said. "You can fly . . ." For a moment One-Note trembled, and everything was still.

Then, suddenly, out of my hands he flew. . . .

As I watched him darting and swooping through the sky, I felt as though I were alongside him, flying with him. I could almost see the world through his eyes, gliding green and falling river blue, and I felt that a bird is like a song in the air, as free as the invisible wind.

It was not long before One-Note and the cats were at it again, and Robespierre was off hiding under his bush, and Madame Footy was shouting at One-Note to stay away from her precious Jacques and Claude.

And, yes, there were times when One-Note flew off and I did not see him for several days. And I knew, as I think you know, that he had found another friend, one with wings.

Then summer was suddenly over. I remember it very well. . . .

I had to pack all my books on my scooter and go back to Paris for a long winter of work at the conservatory.

How could I say good-by to One-Note?

I don't think I ever really did. You can never say good-by to a friend you have come to love.

As I had done so many times before, I scootered down the country road, with One-Note flying overhead, and when we reached the end of the woods, I saw him sail off into his tree. For a long time I watched him, perched up there, with his feathers fluffing in the high breeze.

"I'm not coming back today," I said to One-Note. "Not . . . for a while. Now I must learn how to fly . . . like you."

One-Note chirped into the air, filling the woods with our song. I think he understood; all creatures pure have a way of knowing without being told.

I waved to One-Note, and he flapped his wings. And although the sky was clear, a sudden fall of rain came into my heart as I went to find my way.